The Sound of Colors

A Journey of the Imagination

JIMMY LIAO

English text adapted by

SARAH L. THOMSON

 LITTLE, BROWN AND COMPANY

New York ∾ Boston ∾ London

A year ago
I began to notice
that my sight was slipping away.
I sat at home alone
and felt the darkness settle around me.
But today I walked outside
into the thin gray rain
and made my way to the subway.
I have a journey to go on.
There are some things
I need to find.

I walk down, down, down,
to the subway platform

where the wind never blows
and the rain never falls.

Waiting for the train,
I start to wonder
if all the subway tracks
in the world

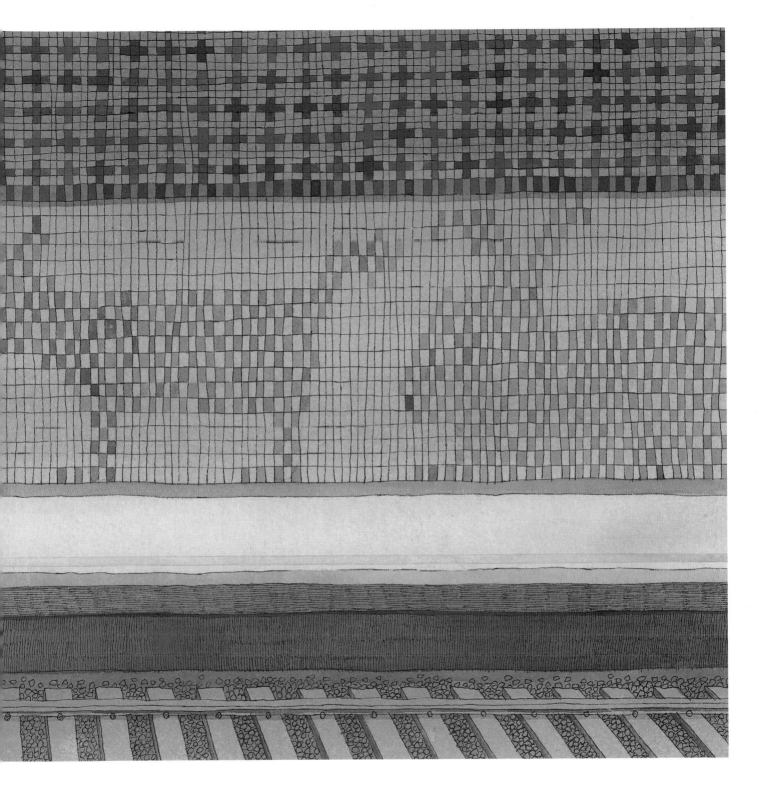

join together.
Then where would I go?

Anywhere I can imagine.

I push my way
onto a train full of people.
Do they all have someone waiting for them
at the other end?

The train shudders to a stop.
The doors slide open.
I don't remember what
this station looks like.
What will be around me
when I step outside?

I climb the stairs
toward the exit,
careful that I don't trip and fall.

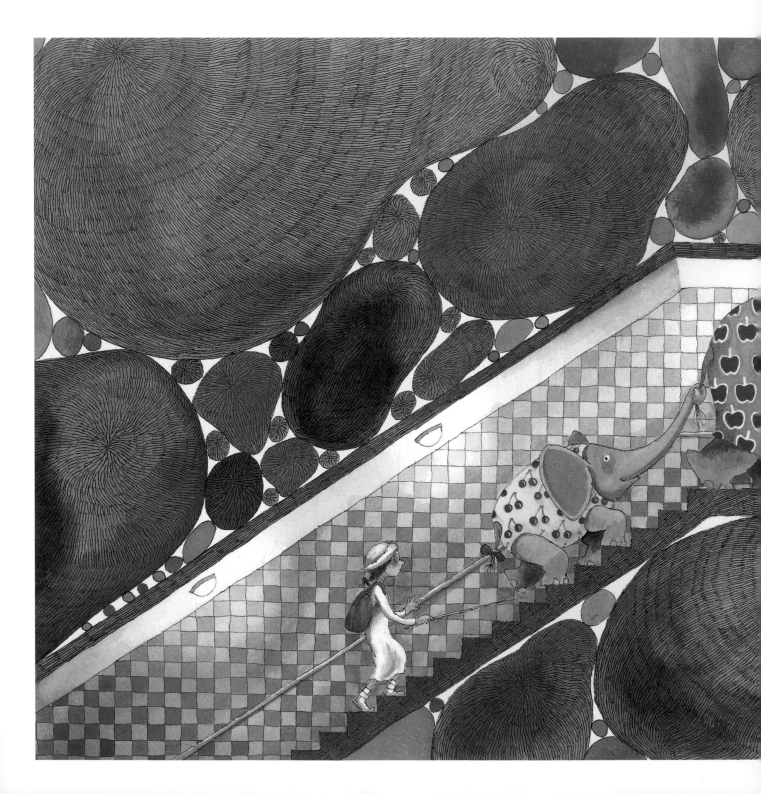

As slowly as an elephant,
I plod up and up,
peacefully, patiently,
one step at a time.

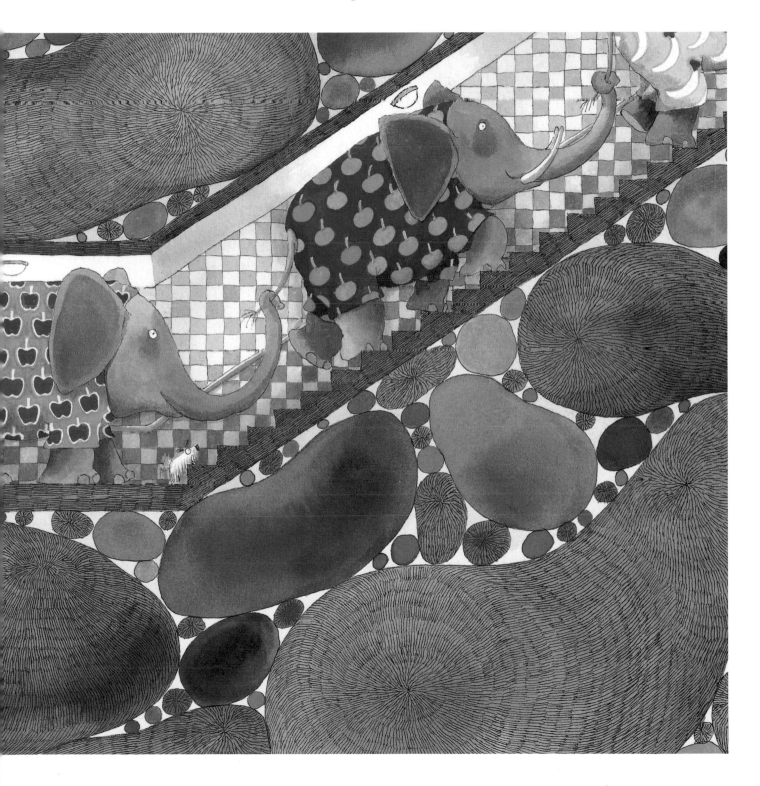

When at last I walk out of the tunnel
I can't see the light,
but I can feel the leaves
falling like sunshine all around me.

I've heard a story
that somewhere nearby
one golden leaf is buried.

I want to pick some apples,
heavy in my hands with their juice.

They'll smell sweet and red.
They'll taste plump and round.

Back underground,
the train scoops me up

and, like a memory,
carries me along.

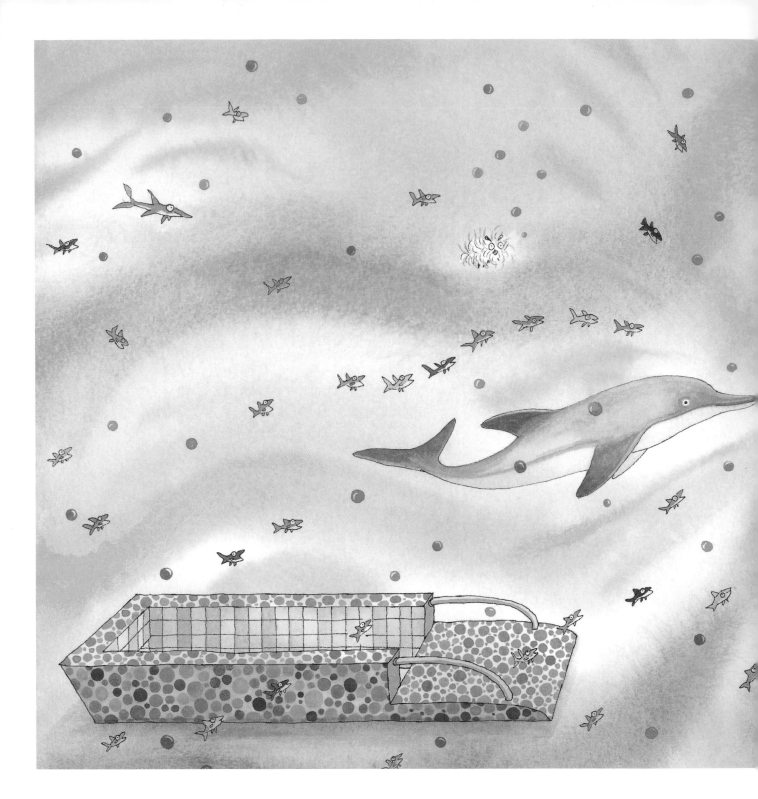

A new station.
Up the stairs again.
What if I stepped out
into an ocean?

I dream that I know
the language of dolphins,
that I can hear the secrets of the sea.

I've forgotten how blue the sky can be.
But in my mind I still
watch the clouds change shape.

I never noticed before
that the train in the tunnel

sounds like waves
against a distant shore.

I wonder what would happen
if I stepped off the last stair
and found nothing beneath my foot.

Maybe the air
would teach me to fly,
just like it teaches the birds,

and the wind would blow me
back to the trains

and set me gently down.

Sometimes, the streets
twist themselves into a maze.

But if you look hard enough,
there's always a way out.

I'll never know if this station
is the same as it was yesterday.

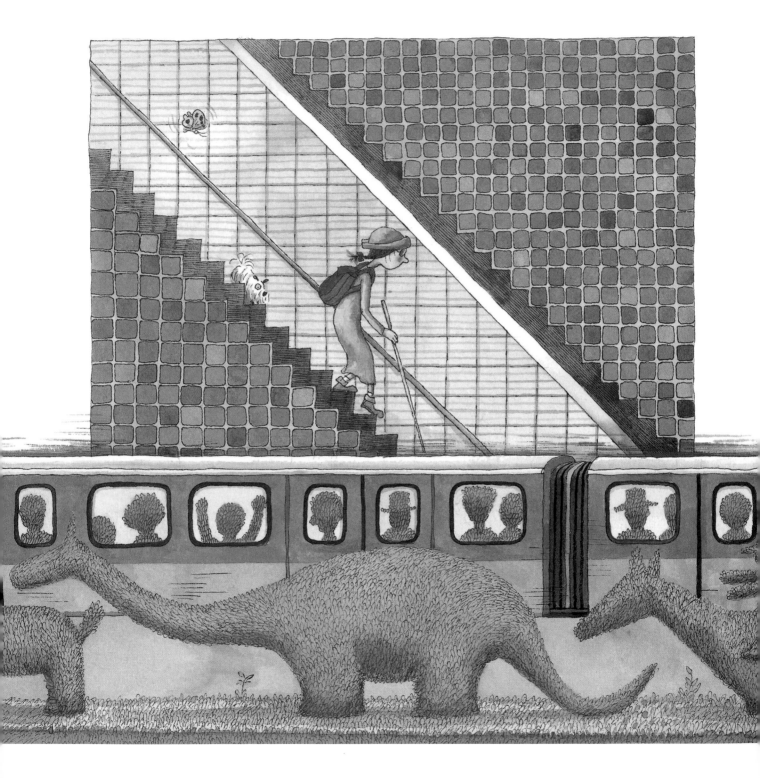

Did it change overnight?
Grow into something new?

Maybe I've come
to the last station
in the world.

But this can't be
the end of my journey.
I haven't found
what I need.

Trains rumble and clank
and rush past me.

Which is the right one?
It's easy to get lost
underground.

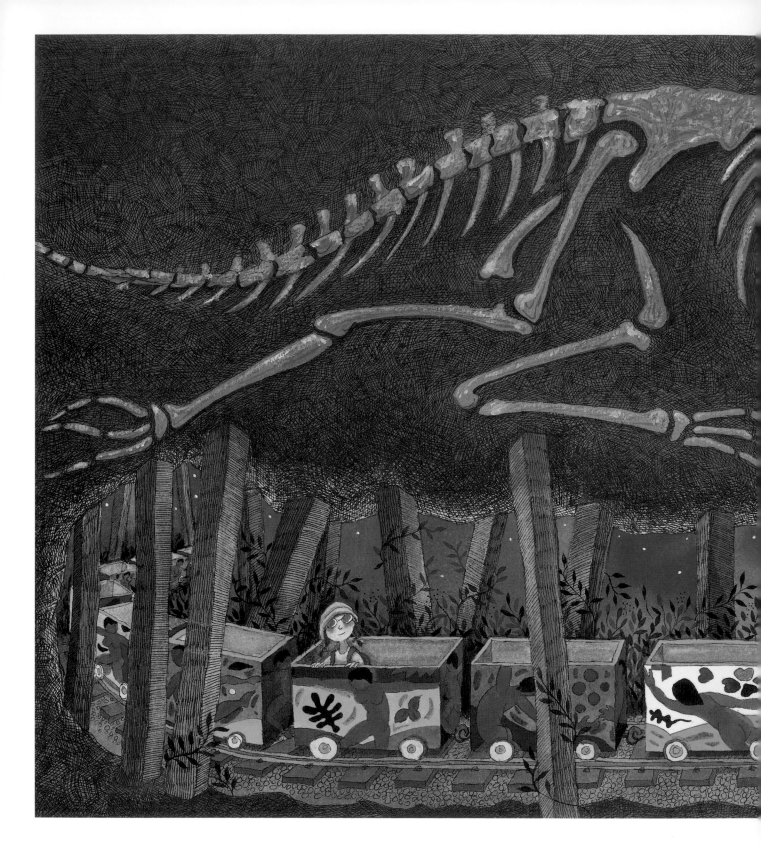

I wonder where I am
and where I'm going,

and if I'm getting closer
to what I'm searching for.

A little boy asks me
how to get home.

"I'm looking, too," I tell him.

Home is the place
where everything I've lost
is waiting patiently

for me
to find my way back.

The last thing I lost
was the light,
as if somebody
played a joke on me,
turned off the switch.

I tried and tried,
but I couldn't find it again.

So I went forward, step by step,
into the dark.

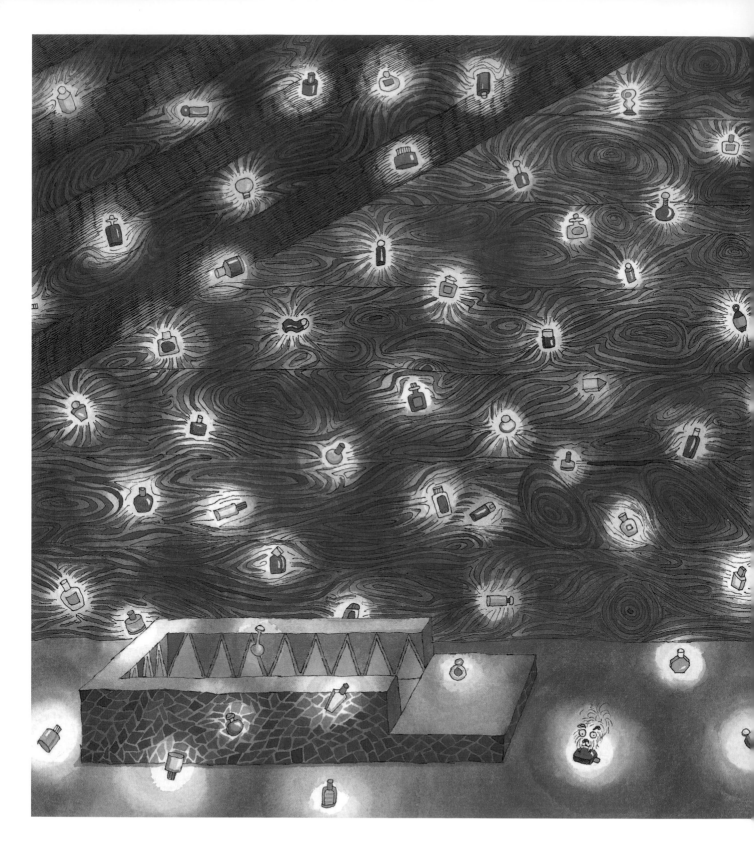

Now I listen for the sound
of the colors I can't see.

I try to smell the shapes,
taste the light and dark.

And I hope to find a friend
who will read me a poem

while the window
fills up with sunset.

There must be someone
who'll sit beside me,
sip tea,
tell me her hopes for the future,
and listen to mine.

Even when I'm tired
of the jolting trains
and the stairs up and down,

one thought keeps me going—
someone could be waiting for me
at the other end.

He'll take my hand
and hold the umbrella over me.
He'll tell me what the stars look like.

He'll walk by my side
all night long.

Listen! Far ahead, at the end of the tunnel,
can you hear it?
A butterfly is flapping her wings.
I can feel the wind she makes
brushing against my face.

I follow her,
going down against up,
up against down,

straining to hear the delicate sound
of her flight
through the clamor of the city

because I think she can show me
where I could find

a juicy red apple
or a single golden leaf.

She'll take me
to the friend I need to find.
She'll lead me to the place
where all the colors are.

She'll bring me back
to the light that I lost,
still glowing here,

in my heart.

JIMMY LIAO was born in Taipei, Taiwan, and received a degree in design from the Chinese Culture University. He worked as an illustrator in the advertising industry for twelve years, but he left to pursue his own creative endeavors. He is the author and illustrator of over twenty hugely popular books that have been translated into English, French, German, Greek, Japanese, Korean, and Thai. *The Sound of Colors* has been adapted into a stage play as well as a motion picture produced by award-winning Hong Kong filmmaker Wong Kar Wai.

Jimmy has said that he expresses the way he views the world through his paintings; looking at his work is like seeing into his heart. A cancer survivor, he hopes that his work can brighten the lives of others. He lives in Taipei, Taiwan, with his wife and daughter.

To Zozo, my little girl

Little, Brown and Company

Hachette Book Group USA
1271 Avenue of the Americas, New York, NY 10020
Visit our Web site at www.lb-kids.com

First U.S. Edition: March 2006

Library of Congress Cataloging-in-Publication Data

Thomson, Sarah L.
 The sound of colors : a journey of the imagination / by Jimmy Liao ;
English text adapted by Sarah L. Thomson.— 1st U.S. ed.
   p. cm.
 Summary: A young woman losing her vision rides the subway with her
dog in search of emotional healing.
 ISBN 0-316-93992-7
 [1. Blind—Fiction. 2. People with disabilities—Fiction.] I. Jimi. II. Title.
PZ7.T378So 2005
[Fic]—dc22   2004025100

10 9 8 7 6 5 4 3 2

IM

Printed in China

The illustrations for this book were done in watercolor.
The text was set in Diotima, and the display type is Naniara.